This book belongs to:

_____

_____

_____

To my daughter Anna,

Who wanted one of Santa's reindeer for her birthday.

NEVER LET A UNICORN MEET A REINDEER!

Written & Illustrated
by Diane Alber

I really wanted a reindeer for my birthday, but not just any reindeer. I WANTED ONE OF SANTA'S REINDEER!

I figured since it's summer, Santa could just have one of his reindeer come and visit and then she could go back in time for Christmas.

But there was just one problem...

How would I get a hold of Santa?

In the middle of summer?

So I did the only thing I could think of...

I quickly put it in the mailbox and
hoped for the best!

It was the day of my birthday. I had a reindeer party theme and even a reindeer welcome sign!
But not ONE reindeer!

Just when I thought it was hopeless,

I heard a knock at the door!

Could this be true??? Did I actually get a reindeer?
And there was a letter, too!

Dear Reindeer Fan,
I'm so glad you wrote me! The reindeer are always looking for something to do during the summer! This is Kiki. She likes to eat carrots and listen to Christmas Songs. But please... whatever you do...

DON'T LET HER MEET ANY UNICORNS!

Sincerely,

Santa

Why would Santa say such a thing?

Unicorns get along with every animal!

Maybe he didn't mean MY unicorn?

Maybe he meant WILD unicorns?

Within seconds, my unicorn came rushing down
the hall and was face to face with Kiki!

I was hoping they would be the best of friends.

Unfortunately, I was so wrong...

Turns out these two were very competitive!
On the first day, it started with whose horns were better...

The next week, they tried to see who could fly better...

Not long after that, they compared their donut
stacking skills!

This went on all the way until December!

It was driving me BANANAS!

Then I heard an envelope
fly under the door...

I opened the door but no one was there!
It looked like it was another letter from Santa.

Dear Reindeer Fan,

We have a big problem and I'm hoping you can help! There is supposed to be a big storm coming in on Christmas Eve and usually I have one of my reindeer light the way, but I don't think it will be enough light for the dark clouds. I'm really getting worried, If I don't come up with a solution soon, I won't be able to see where I'm going, and all the kids won't get presents! Do you have any ideas?

Sincerely,

Santa

Oh no! We have to help Santa! There is only a week before Christmas!

What can we do?

Kiki remembered how Unicorn had made her crayon scribbles sparkle so bright and how amazingly she could fly.

UNICORN COULD HELP SAVE CHRISTMAS!

Kiki told Unicorn that she thought her sparkling scribbles could light the way and create a path for Santa. She hoped that Unicorn would come back to the North Pole with her.

Unicorn loved the idea and the two of them quickly flew off into the night.

A week had passed and I couldn't wait to wake up on Christmas morning. To my surprise Unicorn AND Kiki were waiting for me by the tree. I couldn't believe it! They pointed to the amazing rainbow outside and told me all about their adventures and how they saved Christmas!

It seems like these two truly became best friends after all!

I never found out why Santa didn't want his reindeer to meet a unicorn. Maybe it was because they are super competitive. Either way, now you know if you see a rainbow on Christmas morning, you'll know a unicorn met a reindeer!

Made in the USA
Middletown, DE
17 December 2020